"Our mistress gave me word that she'd discovered us a new companion, that a mountain maid would follow anon. Are you she?"

Phoebe hardly knew how to answer. The goddess had said, "Come!" and Phoebe had obeyed. But there'd been no explanations or agreements.

"She summoned me." Phoebe felt herself flushing and shrugged her long hair over her shoulders, a golden cloak to hide behind.

"Of course!" said the dark girl. "That is how it begins. Always." She proffered the satiny green garment she carried—a peplos and its sashes. "May I help you with this? A gift from the dryads who serve our mistress?"

It was well that such help was offered. Phoebe could never have managed the intricate folds and complex arrangement of sashes alone. Once the dark nymph finished draping Phoebe, she introduced herself—"I'm Aricina."

Also by J.M. Ney-Grimm

NORTH-LANDS STORIES

Troll-magic

Hunting Wild

MYTHIC TALES

Blood Silver

Caught in Amber

Devouring Light

Fate's Door

KAUNIS CLAN SAGA

Sarvet's Wanderyar

Livli's Gift

Winter Glory

LODESTONE TALES

A Talisman Arcane

The Tally Master

Sovereign Night

Skies of Navarys

SHORT STORIES

"Eurydice in Truth"

"Take from Hell"

"To Haunt the Daring Place"

"Were It Only Exile as Promised"

"Faerie Tithe"

"The Hunt of the Unicorn"

"Titan Invictus"

"Blood Falchion"

"The Smith and the Hermit"

"The Kite Climber"

"Right, Wrong, and Amazing"

"Read-Only Memory"

"Serpent's Foe"

"Crossing the Naiad"

"Perilous Chance"

"Resonant Bronze"

"Rainbow's Lodestone"

"Star-drake"

"The Troll's Belt"

COLLECTIONS

A Knot of Trolls

Tales of Old Giralliya

Mythic Tales

Kaunis Clan Saga

THE HADES CYCLE

Tale One

by *J.M. Ney-Grimm*

Wild
Unicorn

Book design by JMNG

Interior Illustration:
"Ancient Greek Charioteer" by Evgenii Kazantsev, Dreamstime.com

Cover design by James, GoOnWrite.com

In memory of
Miss Lynch,
teacher of European history
and great friend to culture and the arts

Eurydice Otherwise

PHOEBE CLOSED HER EYES and dipped her nose into the bouquet of chamomile and poppies. A light apple scent, anchored with earthy notes, bathed her face. She breathed in the perfume—glorious. The delicate stems felt fragile in her fingers. The merry yellow-and-white of the daisy-like chamomile and the scarlet poppy petals formed a mosaic in her mind's eye.

If only she could stay like this forever, crouched gathering flowers at the edge of a sunny glade within a mountain forest. Never no mind that her calves were cramping while the overlong *peplos* tightened around her knees.

This was *her* glade, the glade where her spirit had coalesced, the glade where Artemis had found her, the glade she had left to join the goddess' retinue.

She should never have left.

But the goddess shone like her brother Phoebus—the sun himself—beguiling a poor nymph like a honeybee summoned by poppies to explore the feathery stamens gracing their centers. Phoebe could never have said no. She *hadn't* said no. She'd not known she needed to.

But, oh, she should have.

Just as she should not be picking this bouquet, here and now. Nor should she be picking it for the reason she did. Especially should she not be picking it for the one who had requested it of her.

She *could* stop.

She could pass by the cyclamen peeping with its heart-shaped leaves below the tree where she crouched, forego its sweet lily-like perfume; she could skip the iris and wild violets likewise, scatter the blooms she'd gathered thus far.

It would be safer. She *should* stop. Except she couldn't.

And she'd promised. If she failed of her promise to . . . him, she'd never escape her tormenters. She'd never imagined her sister nymphs could be so cruel. They'd seemed kind at first—well, almost at first—new friends with whom she could play by day, whisper secrets with at eventide, share dreams within slumber. Do all the things that solitude could not permit.

She'd neither known nor missed friends in her birth glade. The sun's warmth, the skittishness of the breeze, the brightness of the flowers and the glory of their aroma, the sheltering arms of the surrounding tree boughs had seemed enough, more than enough.

Her first glimpse of Artemis had banished her content. The keenness of the divine glance, the music of her voice, the gentle power of her touch—all put the sun and scent and sheltering shadows of Phoebe's glade to shame.

She'd left without a second thought, following Artemis as she flitted between the tree boles— following and following, losing her way, catching her long golden locks on thorns, despairing, and then taking new heart as she glimpsed the goddess in the distance.

When Phoebe reached the far meadow in the valley, Artemis was long gone. But her handmaidens awaited. All in a group they stood, silver tresses cascading over shoulders and limbs. They had offered no kind welcome—beautiful faces disdainful, eyebrows raised, collective gaze cold.

In that frozen moment, Phoebe had realized her nakedness, for the moon maidens went clothed in more than their silver hair. Graceful tunics—*peploi*—secured with criss-crossing sashes and waist girdles gave the nymphs a dignity and stature before which Phoebe quailed. Almost did she run fleeing back to her glade. Would that she had.

A dark-haired nymph shouldered forward from behind her pale compatriots. Twisted willow fronds restrained her tumbled curls. Her eyes were hazel and bright. She reached an arm forward as she spoke, voice warm. A silken drape of green fabric spilled over her elbow.

"Our mistress gave me word that she'd discovered us a new companion, that a mountain maid would follow anon. Are you she?"

Phoebe had hardly known how to answer. The goddess had said, "Come!" and Phoebe had obeyed. But there'd been no explanations or agreements.

"She summoned me." Phoebe felt herself flushing and shrugged her long hair over her shoulders, a golden cloak to hide behind.

"Of course!" said the dark girl. "That is how it begins. Always." She proffered the satiny green garment she carried—a peplos and its sashes. "May I help you with this? A gift from the dryads who serve our mistress?"

It was well that such help was offered. Phoebe could never have managed the intricate folds and complex arrangement of sashes alone. Once the dark nymph finished draping Phoebe, she introduced herself—"I'm Aricina"—and then went on down the line of the rest. Oddly, she did not ask Phoebe's name; nor did the others inquire, not even once during the frolic that ensued.

It was days before Artemis returned, but her handmaidens were not dull without her. Phoebe had never smiled so much in such a short time. They summoned satyrs to play panpipes for dancing. They feasted on fruits and wines brought by dryads. They played guessing games. They bathed in the river beyond the standing stones in a farther meadow.

Aricina explained that the stones weren't really a temple or even a shrine.

"Mortals build temples to house the goddess' priestesses, to provide an altar for sacrifices, and a treasury for gifts. They require enclosure, which our mistress could never bear for herself."

Indeed, Phoebe could see that Artemis' sanctuary was very different from the walled and roofed stone structure—surrounded by columns and raised on a stepped plinth—that Aricina described as a temple of men.

The standing stones in Artemis' meadow—tall as tree trunks, but rectangular—formed parallel colonnades along the sides and a series of linteled doorways down the center, while fallen oblongs provided seating.

"Our mistress loves the rain and the sun, the moonlight and the starshine. To shut herself away from the elements would be madness!" said Aricina.

Phoebe had nodded, then frowned in puzzlement. She craved all that fell from the heavens and had never envisioned being closed away from such manna. How could it be otherwise with Artemis, divinity of the lunar orb and the wilds?

All the fun of new friends and new activities ended when Artemis arrived.

Not that the goddess proved a stern task master. Her requests to her handmaidens included the care of her hunting dogs, participation in shooting contests with bow and arrow, running foot races, and accompanying the goddess on the hunt. The party became more varied than ever.

But Artemis introduced Phoebe all over again. By name.

Aricina's face, so bright a moment before, shuttered on the instant. Her lips moved silently. "Phoebe?"

The rest of the nymphs, when they noticed Aricina's reaction, followed her lead. Backs were turned, chins raised and noses looked down, glances cast sidelong. When they visited the dryads, they took care to slip away without Phoebe. When they brushed the hounds in pairs, they left Phoebe a dog to herself. When they danced in double rings, each avoided touching Phoebe's hand as she passed.

It took her some effort to achieve speech with Aricina, so elusive did her former friend become.

"What have I done wrong?" she pleaded.

Aricina's face was stone. "You really don't know?" The nymph's nostrils flared.

Phoebe shook her head. She couldn't imagine that she *had* done wrong, but she must have. Unwittingly. Unintentionally. Meaning no harm. Surely they would not shun her without reason.

"You've done nothing wrong," said Aricina coldly. "You *are* wrong."

Phoebe's stomach felt hollow. "What can I do? How can I atone?" she begged.

Aricina turned away. "You can't," she tossed over her shoulder.

Phoebe had sought her favorite hound—Laelaps— and wept into the beast's fur. Laelaps licked her face once Phoebe's tears subsided.

She learned what her offense was one day while she floated in a rock-bound pool upstream from the cascade where the nymphs rode river currents down a shallow staircase of ripples. The water felt deliciously cool on her limbs, buoying her up even while desolation weighed her heart. The sun warmed her face, a strong contrast to the coldness in her belly. The babble of the chirling eddies muted the happy shrieks of the nymphs as they splashed and dove.

Phoebe drifted, unable to revisit her former joys in solitude, but escaping outright misery for a time.

Eventually the handmaidens tired and gathered on the riverbank to rest, unaware of Phoebe's presence.

"Our mistress should have given her another name," murmured one, low-voiced. "Bibiana or Calixte, maybe."

"Not Calixte," objected a high-pitched nymph. "That means 'very beautiful' and she's certainly not that."

Phoebe knitted her brows. They objected to her *name*? Why? That made no sense. How could her name generate such hatred?

"Amathis"—*ignorant*—"would do," suggested someone with a guffaw.

The nymphs giggled.

Phoebe swallowed hard. Perhaps if they'd not been so friendly those first few days, eager to win her liking, their scorn might not hurt so much now. But they had, and it did. *My name means 'bright one,'* she reminded herself, *and Artemis herself told me that I was bright, like my hair.*

"Really, it's too bad," said a more controlled voice. "You were the only one to bear one of our lady's own names. It's not right that anyone else should be so honored. Iola is close to Isora, but our lady is never just Isora. She's always *Artemis* Isora. And Larissa isn't anywhere close to Locheia."

Abruptly Phoebe put the pieces together.

Artemis was renowned as the 'Goddess of Many Names,' a request she had made of her father Zeus when but a child. And he'd granted it.

Aeginaea, Artemis *Lygodesma*, Lady of the Lake.

Aetole, *Potnia Theron*, Kourotrophos.

Cynthia, Amarynthia, Artemis *Anaitis*, Astrateias.

And—yes— Locheia, as one of her handmaidens had mentioned, patron of midwives and childbirth.

But the most important of all the goddess' numerous epithets, the most honored one—the one that had impelled the youngling to insist she possess many, so as to distinguish her—was Phoebe, the feminine form of her brother Apollo's Phoebus.

And the heart of Phoebe's own trouble was the name Artemis *Tauropolos,* the goddess of the bulls, worshipped in Tauris as *Aricina.*

Before Phoebe's arrival, the nymph Aricina had been the only handmaiden blessed with one of the goddess' names, and now Phoebe herself bore a more glorious one. How . . . petty. Almost did she wish that Artemis had named her anew. Phaedra. Philantha. Or even Phillipa. And yet . . .

Phoebe *was* her name. It had coalesced with her being, there in her birth glade. And Artemis had *not* renamed her.

She wondered briefly if there were anything she might do to regain Aricina's liking, and then discarded the notion. She refused to woo a friend who would choose to treat someone as Aricina had treated her.

Could she request leave to be severed from the goddess' retinue? The question surfaced only to be dismissed. Artemis would honor such a request, Phoebe was sure. But Phoebe could not bear to make it. The friendship of the handmaidens, experienced for just those few days, had changed everything. Phoebe would never again rest so content in solitude as she had before she'd known companionship. And yet that was not the mainstay of her reluctance. It was Artemis herself.

The handmaidens had made life richer. The pastimes within the goddess' retinue had made life jolly. These lesser things were the conscious focus of Phoebe's thoughts. But Artemis herself formed the unconscious foundation of Phoebe's being. She embodied the day's light in the dawning, the moon's radiance by night, the air's softness at eventide, and the solidity of the ground beneath Phoebe's feet. Phoebe could not do without her. No matter how much happier she might be back in her glade, no matter how miserable she might be in the goddess' meadow sanctuary, she must remain.

The handmaidens did not grow any kinder, but Phoebe found herself more able to withstand their shunning, their scorn, their occasional taunts, and their elbows to her ribs. Knowing the origin of their contempt, knowing that she need expect nothing else, did help. She feasted instead on the sustenance of Artemis' presence.

So long as she sat at the goddess' feet repairing her arrows' fletching, walked in her wake admiring the woodland beauties, hid in concealment with her to watch deer at play, or chased after her on the hunt, Phoebe felt joy.

When Artemis was occupied at a distance, it was harder.

And the days and dawns when Artemis was absent altogether—away on divine business or visiting Apollo—were the hardest.

Then, indeed, Phoebe thought of requesting permission to remove to her birth glade, or to be transferred elsewhere to serve another goddess altogether, or at least for Artemis' intervention within her own retinue. Yet every time the goddess returned, Phoebe's woes fled and her intention to ask for help fled with them.

One night, when Artemis was summoned to attend the throne of Lord Zeus, Deianira—the level-voiced nymph who had deplored Phoebe's name aloud—gathered all the handmaidens together within a moonlit glade.

"You, too," she said to Phoebe, glancing sidelong.

Phoebe considered slipping away. That worked well when the others weren't paying attention, less well—or not at all—when they were. She'd learned the hard way to stay far from the river when the nymphs bathed en masse. She'd have drowned without the surreptitious aid of the shy spirit of a grotto located behind a waterfall upstream.

As Phoebe hesitated, Deianira grabbed her wrist and drew her into the circle.

Phoebe suppressed a grimace. Best to comply; resistance would merely heighten her tormenters' determination and enjoyment.

The nymphs settled within a small, pine-edged clearing, and Deianira began. "I have news," she said.

"From Hillary?" someone asked, tone mocking. "Or Lysander?"

The group giggled.

Deianira straightened and smiled. "From Hermes himself!"

"Ooh!" murmured her audience.

"A new winged creature has come from the farthest west, from over the waves, from the trees at world's end, and what do you think is the sound of its call?"

Deianira looked expectant in the moonlight, but she'd not prepared her listeners adequately, and they had no idea how to respond.

"Does it matter?" came a query from the shadows.

Deianira sat straighter yet. "Oh, it matters, indeed. Look at her, so proud in her name, but undeservedly." Deianira tossed her head, pointing at Phoebe. Phoebe willed herself not to shrink. "'Tis not our lady's mantle she bears, nor even that of our lady's brother. No, indeed!" Deianira laughed. "'Tis one small, brown bird. A timid bird. Listen!"

Deianira pursed her lips to whistle, a low note followed by a higher. *"Pho-phee."*

In the shadows, someone began to laugh, gently at first, then louder as she stood and came into the moonlight. It was Aricina.

"How perfect," she said. *"Pho-phee. Pho-phee. Pho-phee."* Her whistle echoed that of Deianira, low-high, low-high. "Fee fee. Feefee. She was always Feefee. How could we ever have been mistaken?" She dissolved into chuckles once more, and the rest of the nymphs joined her.

"Feefee! Feefee! Feefee!" they chanted.

Phoebe sat frozen. Her name. *Her* name, turned from divinity to a birdcall. She felt as though she *should* be strong enough to hold onto an inner dignity that would care nothing for the jibes of girls small enough to stoop to them. But somehow . . . she couldn't.

Deianira jumped to her feet to meet Aricina's reaching hands. The two twirled in an impromptu dance, and then broke apart for Deianira to haul Phoebe up and shove her into the next bunch of nymphs rising to join the celebration. They caught her, whirled her in a dizzying spin, and shoved her back.

The next moments were a blur as she struggled to keep her stumbling feet under her and to hold her head and neck against whiplash as the handmaidens slung her from one to another. They desisted only when the disorientation pushed her stomach to revolt.

"Eew!"

And then they scattered.

Phoebe found herself crying, crouched some distance away beneath ground-hugging pine boughs. The feather touches of the pine needles and their resinous scent calmed her. She would go. She would go to her birth glade until Artemis returned. And then she would ask for help. No matter how joyous she felt in the goddess' presence. No matter how content. No matter how supported. This must not go on.

But her sojourn within her birth glade brought her another choice, wholly unexpected.

She'd intended to embark instantly on the chores of care-taking that made her glade thrive.

She would trim the oleander of its winter-killed branches, prune the myrtle which grew bushy untended, persuade the mint to draw back from strangling the iris, and bless all the baby rabbits born in her absence.

But when she stepped from the dappled shade of the encircling trees into the sunlight of the flower-dotted grasses, she felt so *good* that she did nothing at all.

Except good wasn't really the word for it.

She felt *right*—and strong—in a way that she'd not felt since she left.

The handmaidens' welcome—once they extended it—had made her feel eager. Surprised. Excited. Their games and entertainments, giddy.

Artemis made her energized and capable, but also euphoric, the way Artemis herself seemed at a hunt's successful conclusion.

But the rightness of coming home to her glade showed both the handmaidens and the goddess for something other: powerful influences exterior to her real self. The strength and rightness of her glade was innate, essential, an expression of who she was at heart.

She stood there, drinking it in.

The morning sunlight seemed to flood through her, nourishing her every sinew. The apple scent of the blooming chamomile buoyed her above any care. The warm earth beneath her feet anchored her and supported her.

She would never leave again.

Sinking down, she sat amidst the froth of flowers and grasses, cross-legged, spine straight, face tipped up. The chores could wait. She would fill herself to the brim with *being* here first—with being itself—and *then* set to work.

Gazing up at the blue sky like a benediction, she felt blessed.

Taking in the gentle curve of land cupping her glade, she felt safe.

Breathing in the stillness of the peace surrounding her, she eased down to reclining, eased into . . . slumber.

Even in sleep she retained a subliminal awareness of the glade around her. She seemed to feel the earth turning, while the breeze picked up, and somewhere a bird called.

I should open my eyes, she thought. *Being here is good, caring for it will be even better. I should wake up.*

Even as she strained against the weight of her eyelids, a deep groaning sound—rock against heavy rock—shook the air.

Why did her eyes refuse to open?

The sound came again, grating and reverberant, shaking her very bones. A stallion neighed, fiercely.

Her eyes opened.

From a newly gaping chasm erupted a black chariot drawn by three black steeds. The dark cloak of the helmeted charioteer swirled out behind him as he reined his horses to an abrupt halt.

Phoebe fought the lassitude anchoring her limbs. Why did it feel as though she were wading through deep water?

Then the charioteer stood over her, his eyes glittering through the slits of his face shield, a dark hand extended to help her to her feet.

She knew an impulse to refuse him, but found herself able to do nothing but place her hand in his.

His palm was cool and leathery, his grip strong, and then she was standing, looking up at him.

He pushed his helmet back, revealing his face. His skin was dark, nearly black; his eyes intent and icy blue; his jaw long under its close-cropped beard. Power and mastery seemed to roll from his person. Phoebe nearly fell, so weak did her knees feel. Only his grip kept her on her feet.

"You belong to me, you know," he said, his voice deep and calm.

Her body said this was true, even while her mind insisted that she belonged to Artemis, and her heart protested faintly that she belonged to herself.

"My brother's daughter claimed you while I watched and waited for you to emerge from maidenhood. She misstepped."

Phoebe shivered, uncertain as to the root of her reaction. Desire for him? Fear of him? Repulsion that she'd been watched all unknowing? She wished she could speak. She wished she could say, "Let me go." But her voice seemed absent, her tongue cleaving to the roof of her mouth.

This was Dìs himself, she realized, one of the three greater gods of sky, sea, and stone. Why had she never guessed that the scion of a titan would carry an aura so much more overwhelming than did the children of Zeus? She'd been unable to say no to Artemis, unable to even conceive of it in Artemis' presence. If Dìs wanted her . . . she was his.

"But now it is yours to say to whom you will pledge. I guarded you, but she purloined you, and you assented to that purloining. It is yours to choose whether you will stay with her. Or come to me."

A ghost of a voice inside her pleaded with her to choose herself for herself, but she could not obey it against the ocean surf that was Dìs. Her choice could not be free in his presence.

"Take me," she whispered.

"I have no handmaidens to attend me," he said. "No cupbearers to do my will. But a throne in the deepest crevice of my underworld rests empty and waiting for my queen—it is next to my own—and I shall make the empty seat over to you, if you will it. Do you wish to come?"

She was shaking like a leaf. She could no longer sense any part of her that might resist him, even amidst her terror. Even if she could bring her lips to shape the word no, even as her heart quailed in horror of the dark depths, even as his aura suffocated her, the core of her said yes, oh, yes.

"Why?" she whispered.

His grip on her hand strengthened. "I long for brightness, Bright One," he answered. "The brightness of the day, the brightness of the living. My realm is so very dark."

She shuddered. There would be no rain, no sunlight, no starshine, no heavenly manna falling among the shades of Hades.

"How?" she whispered.

Did his mouth smile? No, it was merely a glimmer behind his ice-blue eyes.

"Gather a bouquet of flowers," he said. "Gather it just for me, only for me. And when the last bloom joins its sisters, then I shall come to claim it as mine. When you give the stems into my hand, when I have placed the stems in the waters of three rivers, then shall I claim you."

"Yes." Her lips formed the word, nearly voiceless.

The whistling call of a mistle thrush sounded in

the distance and then ceased. The very air waited in quietude for some further pledge from her.

"I promise," she said.

He let go of her, and she swayed.

Then he was gone.

She crumpled to the ground.

She lay fainting for an interval, cold with the premonition of what was coming: withdrawal, darkness, death.

I must fight this, I must find some way to escape, some path to freedom.

But how could she fight the god of death, brother to the ruler of Olympus, scion of the titan king Cronos?

She'd pretended she would stay in her birth glade forever more, denying Artemis' claim upon her. Now she knew her pretense for what it was: a glad fantasy that would have evaporated like dew in the noontide's heat when the goddess came to retrieve her strayed nymph. If Phoebe could not withstand even the daughter of Zeus—and she couldn't—she would never stand a chance against his brother.

A tear crept down her cheek, warm and wet and living.

In its wake she noticed the sun's warmth sinking into her bones. The apple scent of chamomile filled her nose. The playful breeze dried her face. She remained yet above ground. Her defeat was not yet. There was still time in which to do . . . something.

A feathery touch tickled her wrist—whiskers?—followed by a velvety caress against her hand.

She opened her eyes to see a baby rabbit nuzzling her fingers.

"Oh!" she exclaimed softly. "I promised I'd bless you!"

And she would.

She had a bouquet to pick. She knew there was no escaping it. She'd promised, and her promise . . . *bound* her. But she would tend her glade first, make up for her neglect these many moons when she had sojourned in Artemis' company, prepare the clearing for the neglectful seasons that must follow her coming departure.

She let her palm drift to the bunny's head, just behind its upstanding ears. "Little harbinger of new life," she murmured, "bless you now and tomorrow, in your comings and your goings, in your refuge and in your meadow, through all the days of your summer, and all the long retreat of winter. Blessed be."

The small creature's eyes shone and its nose twitched. Then it hopped away.

As Phoebe's gaze followed its lolloping gait across the grasses, she noted that her glade was healed of the wound Dìs had dealt to its ground; no chasm gaped there, although the turf showed a more rumpled texture.

Phoebe gathered her feet under her. Would she be able to stand?

Yes. She felt weak in the aftermath of Dìs' visit, but her strength was returning. She regained more as she embarked on her glade-tending chores. The mint's fresh scent gave her a jolt of energy as she weeded it from amidst tender flowers. Blessing a nest of wren eggs and the remaining rabbit babies engendered a bubble of happiness within her.

But the call of Dìs' bouquet grew ever more imperious, and at last she was forced to heed it.

Gather it just for me, only for me, he had said. Very well. She would take him at his word and give him of her best. Her very best.

"May your soul know peace," she said, plucking sunny chamomile.

"May your dead receive honor," she prayed, gathering poppies. "May your kingship partake of generosity."

She buried her nose in the fragrant handful, savoring the chamomile's apple aroma and the earthy notes of the poppies.

"May wisdom guide your search for brightness," she petitioned, amidst the iris, "and faith infuse your spirit."

Chamomile, poppies, and iris—a trio of benevolence, these blooms. How else should she gift him? A spray of arbutus for gratitude? Cyclamen for moderation? Thyme for courage? She herself could use that, because she felt the small beginnings of a plan beneath her thoughts, a way in which she might preserve . . . something.

A scrap of motion flickered in the sky above her.

She looked up.

It soared, dipped, and turned—a bird on the wing, symbol of a soul freed from Hades' hell to fly the heavens of the Elysian Fields.

Ah, she recognized the brown-and-cream speckles of its breast and the taupe of its swift pinions. A mistle thrush flew in the soft breeze sweeping her glade. Did it carry something in its beak?

The bird swooped, gliding toward her, bearing a fragile spray of white poplar. Fluttering in the wind of the bird's passage, the new-budded leaves showed vivid green on their upper sides, bright white on the other.

Phoebe raised her arms in greeting, saluting the thrush with her unfinished bouquet.

The flyer glided closer, backed air with its wings, and bounced onto Phoebe's wrist, claws pricking. Bobbing, the creature stuffed its gift of poplar into the heart of Phoebe's flowers and then darted away, airborne.

Phoebe could only stare at the unexpected offering.

Abele—white poplar—for time and lasting memory. She'd imagined hunting for it—the tree did not grow in her glade—hunting for it, finding it, creating a second bouquet around it for herself and herself alone. A bouquet to anchor her own integrity. But now this creature of the airs had brought her what she sought—what she *needed*—and inserted the gift into the bouquet for Dìs and Dìs alone.

What did it mean? Must she start afresh her flowers for Dìs?

As she stood considering, a murmur of sound drifted from the trees behind her, babbling like the water chattering over stones.

She frowned. No brook flowed there. What was she hearing?

The murmurs grew stronger. Voices—they were nymphs' voices, merry and bright.

"There she is!" came a triumphant call.

And then Artemis' handmaidens swirled around her, their faces mocking and their hands reaching to pull her hair.

Phoebe jerked away, clutching her bouquet to her chest.

Aricina shouldered to the fore. Her dark hair was bound up by silver bands, very like a hairstyle favored by Artemis, and her *peplos* was a short one, the style most convenient for racing and hunting. No doubt she fancied herself as the goddess' true echo.

Aricina's nostrils flared. "Did you really believe you could escape us so easily? Or at all? Our lady never gave you leave to go!" Aricina's hand darted forward.

A slap? A pinch? Another yank on Phoebe's hair?

Phoebe stepped back to avoid it, whatever was intended, and that proved the wrong move.

Aricina's deft fingers plucked the white poplar spray from amidst the flowers in Phoebe's clasp.

"Give it back!" she cried, her voice high and frantic. She needed the poplar! She had no chance against Dìs without it.

Aricina laughed and tossed the branch to another nymph.

Phoebe darted after it, and the nymph tossed the poplar away just before Phoebe's reaching hand touched its bark. One silver-backed leaf brushed her wrist as the spray flew through the air.

Phoebe stopped and swallowed. This was futile. She'd played this losing game so many times before in company of these nymphs. Must she play it once more? She didn't want to.

The handmaidens seemed not to notice that she'd stopped chasing the poplar. They flung it onward from one to another, giggling and calling, "My turn! Throw it to me! Me!"

When it arrived in Aricina's hands once more, however, the head nymph kept hold of the branch, brandishing it before her like a sword. "This precious to you?" she asked, her voice taunting.

Phoebe almost nodded. The poplar was not precious, it was essential, but she refused to acknowledge as much.

Aricina seemed to guess her thought. "Ah! You *need* it. How if I break it?"

A spurt of panic clenched Phoebe's stomach. And then she was angry, too angry to be afraid. Yet she was afraid, but not of Aricina, not anymore. It was Dìs she feared, and he merited fear. Although . . . she found herself wondering, even in this crisis, was any fearful thing truly worthy of fear? Was fear the best response? Surely delving within for strength—as she did now— would yield . . . victory? At least something better than defeat. Or, if defeat, a defeat more honorable than submission.

She stood tall—embracing the rightness of her glade, her birthplace—and gazed at Aricina straightly. "You should be ashamed," she said evenly.

Aricina looked taken aback. Recovering herself, she sniffed. "You're the coward, not me."

Phoebe restrained a smile. She could imagine Aricina whimpering before Dìs. Oh, she had the nymph's measure now. "Perhaps I was cowardly in my dealings with you. Perhaps I should have fought back. But do you honestly believe that you were right to rescind your welcome to me? Would the goddess have been pleased?"

Aricina straightened at this. "Oh! So now you'll be a talebearer and snitch, as well as lily-livered. Ha!"

Phoebe sighed. Why hadn't she turned the tables sooner? Aricina could only prevail so long as her victim quailed. All it took was standing up to the head nymph, and Aricina lost her strength. Phoebe almost felt sorry for her.

Aricina smiled nastily. "Talebearer! Talebearer! You feeble little bird! *Pho-phee, pho-phee, pho-phee!* You'll want to tell, and then you won't even be able to do that! You're a would-be snitch, even worse than a real one!"

Phoebe's pity for this girl strengthened. "No, I've no plans to tell Artemis," she said gently. "I've no need. You fools!" She glanced at the listening nymphs and their chastened expressions. "Do you think it matters whether she knows or not? Think! Your behavior sullies her, even if she never knows of it. She is the protectress of girls and maidens, all women in need. How dare you torment those weaker than yourselves! Each time you do so, you torment those especially under the goddess' wing. You must stop. At once!"

Aricina's face flushed, but she made another attempt to regain mastery. "We've never tormented the weak. Only you! And you're not weak. So there!"

Phoebe felt slightly breathless at Aricina's admission. It was true, she realized. She was not weak, even though she'd allowed herself to be so for too much of her time with the nymphs. She was not weak, especially not here in her birthplace. And yet . . .

"Everyone is weak sometimes," she said.

Aricina's eyes widened, recognizing the words' truth. The handmaiden glanced around herself, still unwilling to surrender, hoping—no doubt—to find support from her cohorts. But it was no good. The other nymphs looked down, twisting their hands and biting their lips. A few were crying.

Aricina took a deep breath. Then she showed her quality, the reason Phoebe had liked her when they'd met so many moons ago. Holding out the poplar spray, Aricina stepped forward, saying, "You're right. Phoebe, I'm so sorry. Will you forgive me?"

Before Phoebe could answer—or accept the poplar—all the handmaidens crowded round her, pleading. "Oh, please, forgive us. Please, don't tell. We'll be better, we promise."

Phoebe stepped back. "I said I'd no plans to tell anyone." Her tone was even, but she wasn't able to say it as gently as she'd intended. She could forgive them, but she couldn't help feeling a residue of resentment. Their willingness to follow Aricina's lead had made her miserable.

Aricina lifted her chin. "But will you forgive them? Will you forgive me? I know . . ." she took a quick breath, "I was the principal in our wrongs."

Phoebe had to admire Aricina's courage. It couldn't be easy owning up to being a bully. But Phoebe wouldn't allow her to shoulder all the blame. "They made their own choices," she said.

Aricina winced.

Phoebe nodded. "But I do forgive them. And you." She stared at each nymph in turn. They wilted under her scrutiny. "Save your regret for the morrow's deeds," she advised. "It does no good to feel badly, if you then go and do the same thing."

All of them winced at that.

"Now give me that branch and go home," Phoebe said.

"But . . ." faltered Aricina, "aren't you coming? Oh, please! Do come and let us make everything up to you!"

Phoebe shook her head. If only she'd done this, confronted them, faced them down, before she'd run away. She could see now that she'd not dealt with them properly. In her heart of hearts, she'd been hoping for their spontaneous approval. Some initiative and a touch of aggression was all it had taken to make them fall in line. Really they'd *needed* her correction. In a way she'd failed them as well as herself. But she was no longer free to follow them and their goddess. She'd made a promise that constrained her by more than her own sense of honor. Promises to a god . . . held the god's power within them.

"I have something I must do," she said.

Aricina's shoulders sagged. "But you'll come after you do it? Please?"

"I may not be free to," Phoebe confessed.

"Oh!" Concern tinged with eagerness suffused Aricina's face. "Do you need help? I can help. *We* can help!" She glanced around her, but the handmaidens looked away. "*I* can help," she repeated.

Phoebe studied the ground a moment, remembering the weakness of her own knees before Dìs, imagining Aricina fainting before the god. No, she would not invite another into danger. Risking herself—as she was bound to—was bad enough.

It occurred to her that this might be the last time she saw Aricina. She hoped she had a chance to survive, a chance at freedom. She hoped the poplar might win her that. But if it didn't . . . Aricina must not depart bearing a burden that could weigh on her forever. Phoebe stepped forward to touch Aricina's hand. She looked the nymph in the eyes, her own gaze serious. "You will lead these girls well. I trust you. The past was an error. You will not make it again."

Aricina's eyes widened. "Let me fetch the goddess," she begged.

Phoebe shook her head.

Aricina pressed the poplar spray into Phoebe's hand. "Goodbye," she whispered, "goodbye," and then she turned away, tears in her eyes.

Phoebe watched as the handmaidens trailed after, following Aricina into the woods, walking slowly between the tree boles, walking until the mountain's downward slope hid them from view.

Phoebe inhaled the scent of the plants she held— the apple aroma of the chamomile a delight, the leathery poplar's odor in her other hand a reassurance.

Must she pick Dìs' bouquet afresh?

No, she decided. *She* had gathered only for him. She would finish his bouquet—*this* bouquet—and learn what it would bring.

And yet . . .

The mistle thrush had found the poplar spray, brought it to her, and even placed it within the bouquet for the dark god. But she could yet omit it. If it nestled at the heart of the chamomile, poppies, and iris, it would be her doing.

Should she toss it away?

No.

She would have sought white poplar for herself. But *he* could surely benefit from the virtues it symbolized: eternity and vivid memory.

She thrust the spray among the chamomile and moved to a sheet of violets, to bless him further. "May you know the contentment of humility," she murmured, gathering beauty like snippets of the evening sky.

Then it was done.

The grating groan of rock on rock sounded. The ground shuddered under her feet. The shriek of an enraged stallion smote the air.

Dìs was here.

She felt his presence in the tidal pull on her bones. *His,* they insisted. *Surrender.*

In her mind, she whimpered for Artemis to come to her rescue.

In her heart, the still small voice of sanity extinguished.

And somewhere beyond all these—hidden somewhere unimaginable—another voice whispered: *I am ready.* Was she?

She heard his steps approach behind her, leather-shod feet trampling the thyme, and the faint clank of bronze on bronze—did he go armored?

She turned, bouquet pressed against her beating breast with both hands. He was close, the face-plate of his helm down, his eyes glittering sinisterly through its eye slits. His dark cloak fell open, revealing a breastplate of blackened metal, leather strips shielding his hips and thighs, and dark bronze greaves sheathing his lower legs. He *did* go armored. Did he fear her?

"Is it mine?" he said, voice deep with strange weight. "All mine?" He gestured at the bouquet—a bright melange of yellow, white, scarlet, and deep blue clutched in her hands, a flutter of green at its core.

Unable to answer, she lifted her face and her flowers toward him.

"Speak," he commanded.

Oh, but she was indeed all his, body, soul, and bouquet.

"Yes," she whispered.

"It is well," he said, accepting her offering and holding the blooms for an instant at his own heart. "When I have bathed these stems in waters from the Styx, the Acheron, and the Lethe, then shall I summon you."

She couldn't imagine how she would come to him, if he did not take her to the underworld himself.

Would the tidal pull on her bones draw her down through the earth of their own weight?

"My summons will be enough," he reassured her, seeming to read her thoughts.

Hating the way she longed to go with him now, she could well believe that his summons would suffice.

He swept his hand with the flowers down by his side, turned away, and left her.

Reins in one skillful hand, he guided the stallions drawing his chariot down the long and steeply winding way to his throne. His other hand held the nymph's bouquet unheeding.

His grip on the stems bruised them.

Down and down he went.

Near to his destination, he halted his steeds at the bottom of a vast crevasse, its cavern ceiling lost in shadows so far overhead that a raindrop, percolating down through Gaia's fields, would fall long enough for a widow to chant the final farewell to her dead before the water hit the cavern floor.

Dìs could see the drop in his mind's eye, cold and unlit, falling, falling, and falling through dark air.

Woe is me, O beloved! You now go beneath the secret

places of the earth, and leave me a sorrowing mourner in your house.

He dismissed his horses to their stables and then descended a spiraling stair through a corkscrew hole in the rock. On the steps' landing knelt a dark figure, head bent. Dìs had told Phoebe that he possessed no cupbearers, and this was true, but he did possess slaves.

Beyond the kneeling slave sat two simple thrones of stone—mere slab seats with slab backs—illuminated by a shaft of light, dull golden and streaming down from some height unseen. The thrones, the pool of light, and a deep tarn of black water formed the pinched base of another soaring crevasse.

"My lord," murmured the slave.

"Is all ready?" asked Dìs.

The slave rose to his feet and moved aside to expose the silhouettes of an urn and three ewers.

"Bring them," said Dìs, walking into the light to stand in the narrow aisle between the thrones and the gleaming surface of the still water. He did not look at the flowers clamped in his grip.

The slave brought the urn first. The light revealed the man to be garbed in a long robe of dark linen. A bronze death mask covered his face. Living mortals might wonder how the man could see, given the lack of eye slits. Dìs knew how—the dead needed no eyes in the kingdom of the dead.

A god needed no eyes there either, but Dìs' face-plate—still down and possessing eye slits nonetheless—made a fit twin to the slave's mask.

"My lord?" said the slave, when Dìs made no move to place his flowers in the urn.

"Lethe first, the waters of forgetfulness," Dìs instructed him.

The man scrambled for the leftmost of the three ewers.

Dìs scrutinized the flowers he held. Already they looked wilted. He extended his arm over the tarn. The slave poured from the ewer, directing the stream to the stem ends. Ripples swept across the tarn's surface where the falling spill plunged, and the sound of water on water echoed loud.

"Enough," said Dìs.

The slave emptied the ewer into the waiting urn.

"Now Acheron and its waters of pain," ordered Dìs.

Another pour, another echo of sound, another sweep of dark ripples, another libation for the urn.

"Now Styx and hatred," said Dìs.

A third inundation.

"You may leave me," murmured Dìs.

The slave knelt. "My lord?"

Dìs studied him silently. "Perhaps it is as well to have a witness," he decided. "Look then."

The man's masked head came up.

Dìs lowered his bouquet gently toward the urn's mouth. Did the blooms look a little brighter? No, they were paler. Less wilted, yes, but losing color.

He plunged the stems in.

Somewhere far overhead breathed an inchoate whisper, like the faintest ghost of a scream.

Phoebe had staggered when Dìs departed, so abrupt was the lessening of his constraint upon her. For an instant, she'd thought herself free entirely. In that heady moment of liberation, she imagined herself loosed altogether from the lord of the dead and choosing her life's course as she wished it to be.

She might return to Artemis.

The compulsion she'd experienced under the goddess was next to nothing compared to the spiritual chains of the goddess' uncle. And the handmaidens' bullying? *Less* than nothing. She'd already put an end to it.

But life in Artemis' retinue was not what she truly wanted.

What *did* she want?

Perhaps she would travel the lands, dipping into different enclaves, trying each until she found the one right for her.

She might go to the ocean's shore and dance with nereids, nymphs of the breaking surf. She could climb to the mountaintops to sing with air sylphs. She might even visit a city of men, live among mortals.

She might.

But, no.

She'd passed through adventure enough.

Gazing across the gentle dell in the mountainside that formed her glade—healed once again of the rift that Dìs had inflicted upon his second coming—she knew what she wanted: *these* grasses, so golden green and dotted with color; *this* clear air and the sunshine, moonlight, and star-gleam that fell through it; the sheltering boughs of *these* trees ringing the meadow; and all the creatures—bunnies, birds, butterflies, and more—who depended upon her guardianship.

But she would need a protector, if she were to stay here.

Even were she free of Dìs as she seemed, she would not stay so in the face of his summons.

Could Artemis serve as the protector of Phoebe's freedom? Surely not. Dìs had claimed Phoebe had a choice, claimed she could choose Artemis over Dìs. But she'd already chosen the wrong way in that decision. And even if she had not . . . would the goddess have *wished* to defy her uncle? Would she truly have consented to release Phoebe from her retinue? Phoebe had believed so in the confines of her own mind, but what did she really know?

But who, if not Artemis?

There was only one real possibility, one entity who possessed power and authority enough to bring Dìs to heel, she realized.

Zeus, King of Olympus.

Even as the god's name crossed her thoughts, she shivered.

When had Zeus ever taken the part of a nymph—or even a goddess—against a desirous male? And when had divine help ever been ought but destructive? She thought of Daphne, turned into a laurel tree when Apollo pursued her; Medusa, given horrific form after Poseidon's transgression; Aphrodite herself, tripped into Hermes' embrace when the eagle of Zeus stole her sandal. The record was not good.

And yet there *were* acts of mercy.

Consider the goddess Leto given refuge by Poseidon on the isle Delos; mortal King Peleus and his bride protected by Hermes from the goddess of discord; the orphaned infant Arcas given by Zeus to the pleiade Maia for succor.

Zeus might not be Phoebe's best option, but he was likely her only one.

Zeus, then.

With the lifting of her chin and the firming of her lips came the deep crack of stone breaking. The earth heaved, Phoebe fought for balance, and then she teetered at the edge of an abyss extending so far down that its nadir lay hidden in shadow.

"No!" she screamed, pushing thin air with frantic hands.

She wobbled back, swayed forward, and lurched back again, falling hard on her side, draped on the very edge of the precipice. Never had the impact of earth against flesh felt so good.

Panting, she tangled her fingers in the grasses to drag herself away from the brink.

A new sensation of sliding, slipping, let her know she was too late. It was not her body slipping into the abyss. It was her soul, her spirit, her very *self* sliding out of her body.

Was *this* Dìs' summons?

She fell, leaving a tangle of golden hair and sun-kissed limbs behind as she plunged past rich loam, arid subsoil, and gray bedrock. Down and down she went. Was she flying or falling?

Pressure built against her belly, breast, and brow, as though her spirit possessed a corporeal weight with which to feel the wind. Like a banner, her hair streamed out behind her.

The sky above, a slit framed by jagged rock, dwindled with impossible speed.

The shadows claimed her.

Down through the darkness she plummeted.

Blacker masses loomed within the stygian gloom—the ghosts of giants? specters of the hydra's nine massive heads? a titan broken free from Tartarus?

Down and down, like a peregrine diving.

Would her spirit shatter at the bottom, broken as bones would break?

The shadows lightened as she flew. Were her eyes adjusting to the dark? Or did a dimly golden glow shine from somewhere far below?

The monstrous hulks she'd feared emerged as pinnacles of rock—red with black veins—rising from unseen depths. Behind her, the precipice flashed past. Craning over her shoulder, she realized it was farther away than she'd guessed when she noticed the narrow thread of a switchbacking path carved from the vertical rock. Down and down it plunged—like herself. Who would traverse such a route, hanging above the impossible abyss?

A waterfall gushed from a tunnel in the cliff to fall beside the descending path.

Down and down and down they three went—Phoebe, glinting water, and sharp-turning path.

Down and down.

The path approached the waterfall.

She caught a brief glimpse of the contrivance that bridged the white froth. An iron chain of massive links draped across the front of the falls, each end anchored within the flanking rock. The chain supported a glass globe, like a bead on a string, and within it a muscled man hauled on the chain to pull the vessel forward. At the far side, a three-headed dog growled and snapped, its beefy shoulder as tall as the ferryman's head.

The tableau was gone in an instant, but the shock of its significance stayed with her. This infinite cascade was the River Styx, the boundary marker of hell.

The golden light brightened, and the pressing wind acquired the scent of burning. Moments later, a torrent of molten stone burst from the rock, swathed in flames and darting downward as a plume of incandescent sparks. She named the fiery fall in her mind: *Phlegethon.* Were all hell's rivers vertical, not horizontal as she'd imagined?

The fiery heat beat against Phoebe like the wind of her fall. Would she burn if she fell too close?

Far below, a caldera protruded from the cliff face to catch the deluge of fire and direct it down a steeply slanting tunnel.

Phoebe prayed she would fall past it. *Let me follow the water, not the fire.*

Even as she completed her prayer, she felt the drag on her inmost self that was Dìs. It was familiar, that pull, and yet it carried a new sensation, almost a draining, as though the vitality of her spirit could be bled from her, just as her spirit had been emptied from her body.

For the first time her fall deviated from straight. She was headed for the fiery caldera and its tunnel outlet.

"No, please, no," she breathed.

There was no time for more.

An instant later, she hurtled into superheated air within the slanting conduit, flaming cataract below, tunnel's rock above. The transition buffeted her like gale winds entering a ravine. Pressure shock compressed her, the hammer of a bronze smith beating her against his anvil. The very air whipping by seemed to burn. Would she calcify like earthenware in a kiln? Would she blaze like torchwood? Or explode into a cloud of smoke that dispersed into nothingness?

Why did she suddenly feel cold, as though she burned amidst ice rather than flame?

The tunnel widened and leveled. She flew across a lake of magma, and then left the fire abruptly behind, tossed out through a breach to fall through the air of another abyss, its stone black streaked with gray.

She'd fallen too fast to fear, and yet she *had* been afraid. Afraid of the fall, the fire, and above all her ultimate fate. But now her fear drove through her like a spike. Did her soul's heart drum within her, as a heart of flesh and blood might pound within a body of bone and brawn? Did her spirit's blood rush through ethereal veins?

This abyss of black and gray—illuminated from above by a rain of dull gold light—was vast, but not so vast as the abyss through which fell the rivers Styx and Phlegethon.

These walls slanted down and in.

How fast would she reach that pinpoint below? How hard would she hit? How painful would her pulping be? How long would her agonized consciousness linger before snuffing out?

The walls narrowed, the pinpoint rushed upward, and then . . . she slowed.

Almost hovering, she gazed down upon a cramped rock rondel with a pool of black water glimmering in a crescent along one wall, its horns embracing a pair of slab thrones. Between the stone seats lay a splotch of paleness, like a clump of dirty sashes.

A dark figure in robes—Dìs, she knew from the draining force he emanated—stood between the thrones and the inky water.

Drifting like thistledown on a breeze, she floated downward to land gently before hell's king. He turned his bronze-masked face toward her.

"Welcome home," he breathed.

The last remnant of her vitality ebbed on his greeting.

She felt cold and faint, as though she might sink through the rock beneath to lie in a sepulcher hollowed by her weakness.

Dìs stood silent before her, not in armor, but ominous in a magnificence different here than in the world above. His dark robe glittered with encrustations of jet, black pearls, black opals, and smoky diamonds. Why did she find it more frightening than his war gear? He still wore his helmet—or, no, he didn't. This was a death mask, not the face-plate of a war helm. She could see a hint of his lips, thin and grim, through the vertical slot below the nose piece, but the eyes were opaque bronze, hiding his living eyes behind the metal. How did he see?

She'd taken his garb as kingly regalia, but it wasn't. He wore funeral vestments, suitable for honoring the dead. Of course.

Was *she* dead?

She glanced down at herself, her spirit form bare of clothing. She'd been here before—naked in front of the clothed—but embarrassment was the least of her concerns. In fact, she didn't care. Were she only clothed in flesh—how she wished she were—that would be garment enough. Did her spirit limbs possess the sun-kissed flush of the body she'd left at the brink of the precipice, that too would suffice. Were her hair golden as it had always been above ground, she would count herself well adorned.

But her limbs shone pale, and her hair lay dead white upon her shoulders.

She lifted her gaze to Dìs, suddenly angry, although no rush of strength accompanied her anger.

She spoke her question. "Am I dead?"

He made an impatient gesture with one hand. "Only mortals die."

"Then I'm lessened. No longer bright, no longer deserving of my name."

"White is bright enough in the dark," he answered, his deep voice calm.

Her anger grew edged, although it felt odd to be furious without the usual physical surge. She wanted to be golden, not white. *I hate you*, she thought, but did not say. Instead, she looked away from him and down, her eyes unfocused on the tumble of dirty white she had earlier taken for laundry.

It was her bouquet.

Every bloom had lost its color. The violets, the iris, the once-bright-yellow centers of the chamomile, even the scarlet poppies were varying hues of white: lilac-shaded white, cream white, rose-tinted white. And the leaves of the poplar spray, stiffly erect, and which should have possessed topsides of vibrant green, showed only silver white.

Her idea for her salvation had failed. She had lost . . . everything.

As she stared, empty and chilling, her bouquet faded further, the ghosts of pastels turning pure white and then going translucent. Transparent. Gossamer.

Was *she* evanescing with her dying offering? Dìs claimed she could not die. Would she drift within his realm as a living ghost instead of a dead one? She felt as transparent as her bouquet, every last remnant of her substance gone.

The last flowers surrounding the poplar spray vanished.

She felt her spirit folding inward and down, as though she collapsed to huddle on the stone floor. Blackness removed even the sight of the lone poplar spray from her vision. Her very will drained from her.

Dìs had said she could not die, but this seemed very like death. She was cold, sightless, unmoving.

And yet . . .

She still possessed awareness. Her spirit felt grief and rage at what had come to her. Her thoughts passed judgement on Dìs for his theft of her. Could she do something when awareness was her only resource?

Oh, but she was cold, and the blackness surrounding her seemed to suck away even awareness, except that it didn't. Amidst the chill and the dark, deep in the very abyss of hell, she remained. *She* remained.

I am, she thought. *I exist. Maybe this darkness is part of me, too.* And if it was part of her . . . then it did not belong to Dìs. And if it did not belong to Dìs . . . she could refuse to allow him to use it.

It was this—she realized—this sucking fear that dwelt at the core of all loneliness that the gods used to fuel their glamor. That glamor promised the end of all loneliness, the end of all want, the end of all insufficiency. Only so long as a mortal—or an immortal—clung to the desire for rescue did the gods have power to promise it.

What if she renounced rescue? What if she *claimed* the darkness, claimed it as *hers,* demanded it as her birthright?

This is mine! she declaimed in the confines of her own mind. Darkness. Fear. Loneliness. The absence of all that life desired. *Mine!*

With that thought, that awareness, she felt Dìs' power fall away. A slight warmth crept into her chill. Coalescing into returning vision, the abandoned poplar spray stood upright and alone in its urn, the silver undersides of the tight leaves pale.

And then—oh! hope reborn!—the leaves of the poplar folded gently outward from their vertical orientation. Their tops were green, vibrant green, and her chance for a miracle—her *own* miracle—had arrived.

She turned to Dìs. "I am not yours!"

"What have you done?" he demanded, his voice grating.

She laughed. "Claimed my darkness, which was never yours." She lifted her chin, knowing that the poplar tree—*white* poplar—possessed attributes antithetical to . . . not Dìs himself, but to death, his jurisdiction. And now the poplar's scion would birth new life. She could hardly imagine how new life would differ from old, but she knew it would be blessed.

Eager, she jerked her gaze back to her bouquet's lone remnant.

The poplar branch was taller, thicker, and growing still. A hairline crack appeared in the urn holding it. The crack widened, and the entire vessel shattered, releasing a mass of roots. The spray was no mere branch, but a sapling, reaching up through the air of the abyss.

Its roots crawled over the two thrones, engulfing seats and backs, then crumbling the slabs to dust.

Phoebe watched in delighted wonder.

Dìs moved to tear the probing roots from their anchorage with his own hands, but then yanked them back as though stung by an asp. "*You* could stop this," he growled.

She could, but the strength of the burgeoning poplar—the tree of remembrance—was now hers. She remembered her power in the confrontation with Aricina and the handmaidens. She remembered her birth. She remembered the fearful core of want. Vitality flooded her.

"I won't," she said.

The poplar roots snaked across the rock of the dais to the pool's brink, where they slithered into the black water.

The sapling was a full-grown tree now, and its leaves rustled in some unfelt breeze.

The pool's water flashed as though struck by the sun. When the glare faded, it reflected the tender blue of a spring sky—the heaven of the Elysian Fields— and then that sky leapt into being, brushed by gauzy clouds. A bird called somewhere, and the breeze ruffling the poplar's leaves caressed Phoebe's face.

A brightness of grasses and flowers spread from the poplar's trunk, mirroring the ripples in the water, passing the boundaries of the rondel that had contained the thrones and racing onward to create the likeness of Phoebe's glade, save for the addition of a woodland pool and the poplar itself.

Dìs knelt, head bent almost as though he were fainting.

Phoebe turned in place, arms upraised, taking it all in, feeling her strength surging. A strand of her hair—golden again, and twirled by the breeze—tickled her wrist, sun-kissed and flushed.

"Poplar is for memory," she murmured, "memory unfailing, memory so intense as to live. I'm *alive*!"

She was living and she was free. She was strong. And no one—not even a god—would ever compel her again.

Her choices lay before her.

THE END

J.M. Ney-Grimm lives with her husband and children in Virginia, just east of the Blue Ridge Mountains. She's learning about zero-carb eating, container gardening, and the discounted benefits of getting vitamin D from exposure to sunlight. The rest of the time she reads Robin McKinley, Diana Wynne Jones, and Lois McMaster Bujold, plays boardgames like Settlers of Catan, *rears her twins, and writes stories set in the magical realms of myth, fantasy, and the far future.*

Look for her novels and novellas at your favorite bookstore—online or on Main Street.

J.M. Ney-Grimm maintains a blog featuring flash fiction from her North-lands and other tidbits unearthed by her ever-active curiosity.

Visit her at http://jmney-grimm.com.